taken by the felon

Emma Bray

chapter
one

Ajax

MY CHEST TIGHTENS PAINFULLY as I watch the live camera feed of my little angel sleeping sweetly in her bed. Her bed is a soft pink with lacy ruffles, and there's a gauzy white canopy hanging down all around it. She sleeps in a beautiful princess bed, looking exactly like a piece of candy at the store that your mother told you you couldn't have, yet you still wanted to reach out and slip it into your pocket when no one was looking, the temptation that you longed to take for yourself even if you knew you couldn't have it.

She's forbidden fruit.

If she was any younger, she'd be jailbait.

Of course, my Olivia isn't jailbait. She's legal—barely legal but legal. I made sure to ask her the first time I laid eyes on her and my cock got harder than a steel rod in my pants.

I've never felt such a potent surge of lust crash through me at the mere sight of a woman. The first time she skipped over to me with that long, honey-colored hair, those innocent blue eyes, and that tight young body that's enough to get me locked back up, precum started leaking out of my cock. That's something that's never happened to me before. Just looking at a woman has never been enough to have me ready to bust all in my pants like an untried schoolboy, but Olivia...

Fuck, Olivia...

She's the prettiest, most perfect little thing I've ever seen.

She'd be worth going to jail for...

Those kinds of thoughts should scare me. I never want to be locked up again. Being in the pen is a bitch.

I roll my shoulders and stretch my arms out in front of me, cracking my knuckles.

I was always buff, but I'm even more muscular now after my stint in the pen. I've always lifted weights, but in prison, there's nothing to do to make the time pass other than work out, which I did incessantly.

My body is a well-honed machine. I know I'm a big,

scary-looking motherfucker, but Olivia—sweet, beautiful Olivia—has never been afraid of me. No, she skipped right up to that fence that separates her house from the lawn I mow and introduced herself and proceeded to chatter away like she didn't have a care in the world—like she couldn't see all the prison tattoos decorating my bare chest and both arms.

She's the first person since I've gotten out who's treated me like a normal human being, who didn't give me wary eyes for being so big and bulky, who didn't immediately look at me like what I am—a felon.

It wasn't hard to slip past her parents' security system and bug the house while they were away. Oh, I have no interest in watching what her parents are doing, but I need to be able to see Olivia at all times so I can make sure she's okay. I of all people know the terrors that can happen to a young girl, even if she thinks she's safe in her own home.

My jaw clenches as I think back on the reason I went to prison in the first place. That's never going to happen to my Olivia. Not on my watch. I might not have been able to protect my sister, but I got vengeance for her.

I know Olivia's parents warned her away from me. I can still remember her father's mask of rage and the suspicious look on his face when he came outside and saw his innocent young daughter talking to me across the fence that separated his yard from his neighbor's.

I knew right then and there that I'd never be cutting his lawn or doing any sort of work for him. The man doesn't want me anywhere near his daughter, and I can't say I really blame the guy based on my criminal record alone. It's only one conviction, but it's a pretty big one. Olivia's father is another one of those who judge without knowing the full story.

Not Olivia, though. She didn't heed her father's warning. No, my pretty little princess kept sneaking out to come talk to me while I worked. It doesn't matter if it's sunny outside or not because her smile is enough to light up my entire world on the gloomiest day. I live for those moments when she comes skipping out the back door and prances over to the fence with that beautiful smile.

God, the first time she said my name in that pretty little voice, I swear I came *this* close to nutting in my pants. I definitely shot a stream of precum. I went home with a stain on my boxers and then jacked off three times in a row to the memory of her voice saying my name.

And that's what she does to me. I don't even have to imagine her naked. I can just picture her little face, remember the way her breathy little voice sounds, and that's enough to have me coming harder than I've ever come in my entire life.

I know she wants me too. I see the way her eyes flick over my shoulders and my bare chest. I see the way she bites her lip when sweat glistens on my skin. I even see the way she smashes those pretty little thighs together like she's trying to ease the ache between them. I'd bet my life the poor baby has never had a proper orgasm before. She might not even know what her body needs, but I sure as hell do, and I'd give my life to give it to her.

My cock is always so hard every time I'm around her. All she has to do is be in my presence, and the fucker is trying to bust through my pants, straining to get to what I already know is an unpopped little cherry, and dammit, that is *my* cherry. It's *mine* to pop.

The thought of another man stuffing his dick between her thighs makes me murderous with rage. I know Olivia feels this pull between us. That's why she disobeyed her father and sneaks out to come speak a few words to me when she sees me working at the house next door.

Olivia is a good girl. She just graduated high school, and she was always a straight-A student. Her parents have it planned for her to go to college, but something tells me that's not what she wants to do. She looks less than enthusiastic when she talks about her future at the university.

Yes, I know she wants me too, but a lifetime of falling in line and doing what her parents have told her to do is holding her back. She might sneak out for a few moments to speak to me across the fence, but she's not brave enough to jump across that line yet. Every time I've asked her to sneak away with me, let me take her out for a bite to eat or a walk in the park or *anything*—anything just to get her alone and spend some time with her without having to look over our shoulders for her parents—she bites her lip, her eyes looking torn and sadly declines, saying that she's sorry but she can't. I can see in her eyes that she truly is.

That's why I don't give her a hard time about it. I've contented myself with watching her from afar and taking whatever crumbs she throws me. I'm like a dog desperate for anything I can get from her. I'll be in her life however I can take it. I'm her silent protector, watching her over the live feeds I have set up in her house, and when she goes out, I'm in the shadows, following an unseen distance behind her to make sure nobody messes with my girl.

And I truly was content with that—until tonight. Until I saw her slip her fingers underneath her little cotton panties. I watched her stroke that little virgin pussy. I could tell she was unsure of what to do, just following her instincts, and god help me, but I couldn't stop myself from pulling my hard cock from my pants and stroking along with her.

I was ready to nut after three pumps, but I held back, only wanting to come when she did, and when she came and whispered my name on her lips, my spend ripped up violently from my balls and shot three feet in the air with my surprise.

Knowing that she was thinking of *me* when she was touching herself, that thoughts of *me* are what ultimately got her off, that's what ultimately sealed my decision. It was a game-changer.

Olivia isn't brave enough to be with me on her own. She's too afraid of disobeying her parents and disappointing them to make that decision on her own.

So, I'll make it for her.

chapter
two

Olivia

I wake up with a gasp when I suddenly feel a huge hand over my mouth. My eyes snap open. I'm awakened out of a dead sleep and instantly alert, which is odd for me because I'm usually a slow waker. I usually have to blink a thousand times for reality to come crashing back down on me, but my eyes instantly home in on a big, hulking figure.

I relax a bit when I recognize the man hovering over me. Ajax. The felon who works for the old lady next door. He cuts her yard and does various other lawn tasks, and even though my father warned me to stay away from him, there's something about the big man. I'm not going to say he reminds me of a big teddy bear or a gentle giant because he exudes an aura of danger.

No, it's something else. I could sense that this man was big and dangerous and scary to other people, but I could also sense that he would never hurt me. I don't know where I get that impression from, but for some reason, I feel safe with him, and the loneliness in his eyes makes me want to talk to him and let him know that he's not alone in this world.

I don't know everything about his record. All I know is my father told me he's a felon, and he's dangerous, and for me to stay away from him. He didn't give me any details. He didn't tell me what he was charged with or convicted of or how long he was in prison. It couldn't have been too long because the man still looks relatively young. I would place him in his early thirties at most, which is certainly older than me. I'm only eighteen. I just graduated high school, but I'd hardly call a man less than forty old.

And good lord, he's in amazing shape. He must spend every day he was locked up working out. The man has nothing but bulging muscles underneath inked skin. He's covered in tattoos, and my fingertips always itch to trace them when I'm in his presence, yet I've never touched him, and he's never touched me.

I think he wants to, though. I see the hunger in his

eyes whenever I talk to him, and maybe that's part of why I keep talking to him. Maybe it's the thrill that it gives me, yet I know it can't go anywhere. Every time he's asked me out, I've declined. Though a part of me wants to see where this can lead, there's that other part of me that's ingrained to listen to my parents. After all, they're my parents. They have my best interests at heart, right?

Yet I still keep sneaking out of the house to talk to Ajax. Maybe I just like flirting with danger. Maybe that's what gives me the thrill more so than anything else. I don't know. All I know is I can't stay away from the darkly handsome, tattooed felon, and now, here he is in my room with his hand over my mouth.

I go completely calm under his hand as my instincts kick in. I can trust him. I don't know how I know that, but I do. He's not going to hurt me.

I see the surprise flicker through his eyes when I still beneath him. Did he expect me to fight him?

He strokes his other hand over my hair soothingly, and the contact sends tingles throughout my scalp. I want to feel his hands skating over the rest of me.

It's amazing how big yet gentle they are. He shushes me even though I haven't made a sound. "I'm not going to hurt you, honey."

I don't know why he's here, and I don't know what his plans are, but I believe that. That's why whenever he emits an apology and pulls a needle out of his pocket, my eyes go wide.

My survival instincts kick in then, and I begin struggling. I didn't think he would hurt me, but now I'm not so sure.

"I'm sorry, honey." His mouth is still moving. He's saying something else, but I don't make out what it is. I'm so focused on the needle. My skin pricks, and as Ajax drugs me with something, the sting of betrayal hurts more than the sting of the needle. I thought I could trust him.

Oh, how wrong I was.

Turns out I should have listened to my father.

***

I wake up slowly. My eyes feel heavy as I blink them, and my vision slowly comes into focus. My brow furrows in confusion when I realize I don't recognize my surroundings.

I sit up quickly as everything comes rushing back to me.

Waking up to Ajax's hand over my mouth. Him telling me 'sorry' as he pricked my neck with a needle.

My head immediately begins to throb, and the world tilts on its axis. I moan and grab my head.

Suddenly, Ajax is right there, steadying me with his hands on my shoulders. He gently pushes me back down so that I'm lounging with my back against the head-board. "Be careful there, honey. Don't sit up so quickly."

To my horror, I feel my body start relaxing at his voice, but then my mind catches up and reminds me I can't trust him, that I should be afraid of him.

I yank my shoulder from his grasp, glaring at him. I still feel the sting of betrayal throbbing in my neck. I subconsciously move my hand up to cover it.

"Where am I?" I ask him.

"Someplace safe," he answers without blinking.

"Did you kidnap me?"

His lips thin at the accusation. "No, I made the deci-sion you're too afraid to make yourself."

I raised an eyebrow at him incredulously. "And what's that?"

He sits on the bed next to me and strokes one of his big fingers down my cheek. His touch burns me, and my breath hitches, but I hold his eyes fearlessly. They're a deep chocolate swirled with caramel, like the most deca-dent dessert.

My eyes trail down over his strong jawline that's lined with stubble. Every time I've seen him—even first thing in the morning—he has a hint of a shadow on his jawline like he has so much testosterone it laughs at his attempt to shave.

The hair on his head is dark and thick. His lips are

unfairly sensuous, lush, and full. He's wearing a black T-shirt that fits him like a second skin. Muscles burst out from underneath the short sleeves that can't contain them. My eyes flick over the tattoos trailing down his arms. I know that they cover his chest and back too from the times I've seen him without his shirt. The image of sweat rolling over the cords of his muscles is permanently burned into my brain.

I realize my gaze has been traveling over him, and I snap my eyes back to his caramel ones that are like melted chocolate. They're heated as they capture mine and he pronounces softly, "I know deep down you want me too."

My breath hitches again at his admission that he wants me. "I know your daddy warned you away from me, and I know you kept sneaking out to talk to me anyway." His lip quirks up into a cocky half-grin before he adds softly, "You're just as drawn to me as I am to you, honey."

I open my mouth to deny it but end up blushing instead. I can't deny what he says. It's all true.

"You wouldn't go out with me," he goes on, "so I took matters into my own hands."

I snort. "So, kidnapping is the next step for you when a woman says no?"

His eyes darken, and his jawline hardens. "You didn't

say no because you don't want me. You said no because you're afraid of disobeying your parents and rocking your perfect little world. If I'm wrong," he splays his hands out, "if I've misread the situation, then tell me here and now. I've never been one to force a woman to do anything, and I won't force you. If I've been wrong about this entire thing, and you want absolutely nothing to do with me, say the word now, and I'll release you."

I bite my lip. He's staring down at me stoically. Ajax drugged me and took me from my bed in the middle of the night, yet he's acting offended when I accuse him of what he did—kidnapping.

I know what I should do. I know what the smart thing to do is. I should deny my attraction to him. I should say whatever it takes for him to let me go.

But...I'd be lying. And the look in his eyes lets me know he knows that too.

So, I press my lips into a stubborn line and look down.

I feel his blunt finger under my chin. He tilts my face up and forces me to meet his eyes again. The look in his eyes is possessive as he trails a thumb over my lower lip and then gently strokes it across my cheek.

He lowers his face until his lips are so close to mine that I can practically feel them skating over them as he whispers, "That's what I thought."

chapter
three

Ajax

"Last Chance, Olivia," I warn her. "Are you sure you don't want me to release you? Because this is the last time I'll ask you. If you change your mind after this, all bets are off." I mean it too. I'm barely holding myself in check by a thread as it is. Once she admits that she wants me, there's no way in hell I'll be physically capable of releasing her.

She'll be mine.

A thrill goes through me at the thought. Olivia as mine is like a rush of adrenaline straight to my system. Mine—and everything that goes with that.

Her cheeks flush, and her lips thin. Her eyes flash with anger.

I can't help the smirk that twists my lips. "You want to do it, don't you? You want to tell me that you don't want me, so I'll release you. You know it's what you should do, but you can't. You can't do it because you know it'd be a lie."

If possible, Olivia's cheeks turn an even brighter red, and my grin widens. Consequently, my cock springs to attention at the confirmation of what I've suspected all along. Try as she might to deny it, try as she might to be daddy's good girl, Olivia wants me too—a low-down felon who in no universe would ever be good enough for her.

The selfish kind of villain who doesn't care and who will take her anyway, though.

Her sweet breath is fanning over my lips, and her sweet honey scent envelopes me. Everything about her is so motherfucking sweet.

"You're going to be the death of me, you know that, honey?" I ask her.

Those blue eyes peer up at me in confusion. "What do you mean?" Her voice comes out in a breathy whisper that has fire roaring through my veins. It calls to mind limbs tangling together in satin, bodies moving together.

"What were you thinking of tonight before you went to bed?" I ask her.

Her breathing hitches and she looks away from me.

I'm having none of that, though. I turn her face back to me. Her skin is petal-soft underneath my fingertips. She's like a flower, so delicate and breakable, and that might should scare me because I'm so big and rough, but it just causes a surge of protectiveness to rise in me.

When she doesn't answer, I lay all my cards on the table. I skate my lips right over her ears as I whisper huskily, "Were you imagining my lips on you when you played with that pretty pink pussy tonight?"

She gasps and jerks back from me. She sputters for a moment before she finally decides there's no use in denying it and instead accuses me, "You were watching me?"

And that's one thing I love about Olivia. She doesn't lie. She's genuine. So far, she hasn't made any half-hearted denials of anything.

Because I can't keep my hands off her anymore, I place them against the small of her back, noticing how one hand spans her entire back. That's how tiny she is in comparison to me. "You bet your sweet ass I watched you play with that pretty little kitty."

She blushes and tries to look down again, but I grab

her chin and force her to meet my eyes when I ask her, "And you know what that means, don't you?"

She bites her lip and tries to look away, but I hold her fast.

My voice is rough as gravel when I say, "I heard you cry out my name when you flooded those little white cotton panties."

"Oh god," she moans in embarrassment, but I shake my head at her as I trail one of my hands around her waist and down to the band of her little pink sleep shorts.

"I bet your little panties are still soaked, aren't they?"

I pause with my fingers barely under the band of her shorts. As much as I'm dying to slip them under her panties, I don't—yet.

Instead, I hold her eyes as I slide my hand down over the cotton until I'm cupping her sweet mound through her panties.

My nostrils flare, and my breathing becomes uneven.

"Soaking fucking wet, sweet baby."

She whimpers, and that sound registers straight in my cock, and I can't hold back any longer.

I crash my lips down onto hers, finally tasting her sweetness. And holy shit, she tastes even sweeter than I imagined she would. She's like pure sugar, and the rush goes straight to my head.

I feel dizzy, especially when her little gasp grants me entrance to her mouth. My tongue forges forward like a ruthless invader, conquering each corner of her sweetness with every swoop of my tongue. I find her tongue and tangle mine with hers. My balls feel heavier than they've ever felt. My cock is so hard it could bust through concrete. Every nerve ending in my body is crackling.

I feel like I've taken a hit of heroin. I'm euphoric, buzzing on Olivia.

And while I'd love nothing more than to make her mine right this instance, especially when she melts against me, she pulls back the tiniest bit too, showing her reluctance.

She desires me, but she's still not all the way there yet. She's going to need time to get used to everything, so as much as it pains me to do so, I force myself to stop kissing her.

I can't stop touching her, though. I stroke my hands over her cheeks and through her long tresses. She closes her eyes and leans into my touch. I bet she doesn't even realize what she's doing. She's practically purring for me.

My throat gets tight with an unfamiliar wash of emotion.

Fuck, this girl. She's everything. I already knew I was

obsessed, but with this one kiss, my obsession has gotten a million times worse.

I feel Olivia trembling in my hold as I lower her to the bed and settle myself next to her.

She seems surprised when I turn her so that she's facing away from me and pull her back against me to spoon with her.

"Ajax," she whispers my name, the confusion and uncertainty clear in her voice.

I shush her for now. "Go to sleep, Olivia."

She stiffens in my hold like she resents being told what to do. She tries to turn in my arms, but I tighten my hold around her when the motion causes her ass to press more firmly against me.

She stills as she no doubt feels me and realizes the situation she's in. I can feel her heart beating a mile a minute, so I set her fears at ease by repeating, "Sleep, Olivia. We'll talk more in the morning."

I'm half relieved and half disappointed when she obeys me.

I lay there for a long time after my angel has slipped into sleep in my arms, looking down at her with a sense of contentment like I've never known before.

My Olivia.

chapter
four

Olivia

When I wake up, I snuggle deeper against the warm body before my eyes snap open as reality comes crashing back in on me. I push back sharply, but a band of steel around my waist tightens and holds me against the chest I was just nuzzling.

"It's amazing how quickly your demeanor switches when you go from a subconscious state to a conscious one." Ajax's deep voice rumbles dryly.

I smile up at him acidly. "I suppose you could always drug me again if what you want is a comatose woman."

Ajax frowns.

I smile smugly when I realize I've gotten the best of

this round. My smile quickly fades when he growls, "What I mean is when you're sleeping, you curl up against me like a sweet little kitten, and then as soon as you wake up and remember you're not supposed to like me, your claws come back out."

"I always liked you," I deny. "You know that. I went against my father's wishes to speak to you."

He raises a knowing eyebrow at me, and I bite my tongue. Dammit. I just proved the point he's been trying to make all along. Which is I want him, but I'm not brave enough to stand up to my parents.

It doesn't matter how attracted I am to him or how much I still love talking to him, though. He's changed the game now. He kidnapped me. I can't be the same way I was.

Right?

He kidnapped me, and I'm supposed to be upset about that.

"You kidnapped me," I speak aloud to both of us, but I think I'm speaking to myself more than anyone, reaffirming the rules of our situation.

"I made the decision you were too afraid to make yourself," he corrects.

We stare at each other—more like I glare at him, and he stares back at me stubbornly.

"I need to pee," I finally say flatly.

He reluctantly releases me, but he gets out of bed with me. I look back over my shoulder when I pick up on the fact that he's following me to the bathroom.

I turn around and cross my arms. "I've got this." I scowl at him.

His lip twitches. "I know you do, honey. I'm just gently reminding you that I'll be right outside the door, so don't try anything." He looks at me pointedly like it's inevitable I'm going to try to escape from the bathroom.

I don't dignify his statement with a response. Instead, I flounce into the bathroom and slam the door in his face. I take care of business, fuming the whole while. I hate feeling like a prisoner. Why did Ajax have to go and ruin everything? I was happy with our flirting. And yes, I used to wonder what it would be like if we could be more, but that was outside the realm of possibility.

My heart clenches when I think of my mother and father. They're going to be so worried. Yes, they're overly protective. They always have been. They've always done their best to shelter me—probably too much. They're both teachers. I'm their only child, and they know what can happen to kids. They've seen it all before in the public school system.

It's ironic that my parents chose to teach in the public school system, yet they insisted I went to a private one. Maybe it's because of everything they saw go down in public schools where they teach. I don't know, but they've always done the best they can to take care of me and give me the best they can. While I might not always agree with them on everything, I do respect them, and I know that they want the best for me.

I'm eighteen now, so technically, I can go anywhere I want and do anything I please, but I can't bear the thought of disappointing them. So, I know that on some level Ajax is right. If I took my parents out of the equation, I'd have gone out with him in a heartbeat.

But I can still see my father's scowl of disapproval. All he had to hear was the word "felon," and that was enough for him to condemn Ajax. Granted, I don't even know what he was in prison for, and he has just kidnapped me, so maybe my dad was onto something there.

Still, something inside me rails against the knowledge that Ajax has been to prison. It tells me that Ajax isn't a danger to me. It wants to give him the benefit of the doubt, even as my mind tells me I cannot give in and be okay with this.

After I take care of business and freshen up, I open the door and find Ajax leaning against the wall. He cuts those brown eyes at me, and I immediately make my demand. "I want to talk to my parents."

He studies me for a long moment before he shocks the hell out of me by nodding. "Okay."

"Okay?" I repeat skeptically.

"Yeah," he tells me with a pointed look. "I know you just want to reassure them that you're safe so that they don't worry about you."

"Aren't you afraid I'm going to tell them I've been kidnapped?"

He grins at me then. "You won't do that. You don't want to put your parents through that."

He closes the distance between us until there's scarcely an inch left between our bodies. "I'm going to let you call them from a burner phone. What you tell them is up to you, but I figure it'll be something along the lines of now that you're eighteen you wanted to spread your wings a little bit. It has nothing to do with either one of them. They're wonderful parents, but you needed to find yourself and for them not to worry and that you forgot your phone at the house. That's why you stopped and picked up a prepaid."

I glare at him, my lips pursed before my shoulders finally slump. He's exactly right. That is what I'm going to tell them because I don't want them to worry. If my dad found out I was kidnapped, it would be on the seven o'clock news. Plus, my dad is friends with many policemen on the police force. There would be a manhunt, and I can already see my mother's tearful face. I know she'd stay awake all the time worried about me.

And they'll probably worry about me still, but it won't be as bad this way. Ajax must read the acceptance in my eyes because he wordlessly walks over to the nightstand, opens the drawer, and pulls out a phone.

My eyes flick to the drawer curiously. Who casually has a burner phone in their nightstand? I'm starting to realize I don't know as much about Ajax as I once thought I did, and a shiver runs down my spine at the thought, though fool that I am, it's not exactly a shiver of fear If I had to describe it, I would say it's more like a thrill of excitement.

I'm obviously fucked in the head.

I make the call to my parents, and while they don't sound happy about the news, I think they accept it. Well, if I know my father, he's going to do a bit of digging. He'll definitely be checking the security system, but something about Ajax's totally relaxed manner lets me know that won't be a problem. If he was smart enough to slip past my dad's security, I'm sure he made sure there'd be no trace of him leaving with me either.

"So now what?" I ask him as I toss the phone onto the bed. "Do you plan on keeping me here forever? What am I going to wear?" I just gesture down to my sleep clothes. "Or do you plan on keeping me locked up in here like this to my dying day?"

Ajax ignores my sarcasm and walks over to the closet. He throws open the door, and my mouth falls open when I see a fully stocked closet. One side is dedicated to his clothes. Another to feminine clothing that I already know is all in my size.

My skin buzzes all over with realization.

"This wasn't some spur-of-the-moment thing. You've been planning this for a while."

Ajax doesn't deny or confirm the accusation. Instead, he walks into the closet and pulls out a pink dress with little red cherries on it. He hands it to me.

I take it, and my immediate thought is that it's beautiful and exactly like something I would have picked out myself. I'll never tell him that, though. Instead, I say snarkily, "What, so you plan on telling me what to wear now?"

He waves his big hand toward the closet. "By all means. I just thought you would like this one."

I do like it.

I look down at the dress and sigh. "Ajax, you can't keep me here forever," I point out.

His lips thin before he says sourly, "Watch me."

My heart leaps into my chest when he pins those chocolate eyes on me and starts taking methodical steps toward me. "I told you, Olivia. Last night was your one chance to leave. You made your choice."

The growl in his voice makes me clench my legs together in response as an ache wells up deep within me.

What the hell is wrong with me? The man is basically telling me he has kidnapped me and my release window has closed. I should be trembling in terror—not clenching my legs to abate my lust.

I swallow and try to redirect. "College will be starting in a few weeks," I point out.

He shrugs, and my eyes catch on the motion of his huge shoulders rolling. "I don't think you really want to go to college, honey."

My face heats. I look down, unable to meet his knowing gaze. How does he know that? I've never told anyone that.

My parents are teachers. It's expected that I'll go to college. They've been prepping me for college since the day I was born. I can't let them down.

I feel a gentle finger under my chin, and then my face is tipped up until I'm looking into chocolate caramel eyes. The expression on Ajax's face softens as he gazes down at me. "If you wanted to go to college, I'd make sure you were there, but this isn't something you want to do. I don't even think you know what you want to do. You've always let your life be dictated by others."

My breath stutters to a stop. I feel exposed. It's like he's looking directly inside me and seeing all the uncomfortable pieces I keep locked up away from the world.

Ajax must have been in prison for theft because he's stolen the key to my soul and unlocked all my secrets without me even realizing it.

I pull my chin out of his grasp and jut it at him. "What do you think this is? You're taking my choice away too. I'm your captive. I'd hardly say I have freedom here with you."

Ajax's jaw ticks before he finally says softly, "I think you'll find out you'll have more freedom here with me than you've ever had in your entire life. I don't want to control you, Olivia." He steps close to me, so close that his lips almost brush mine as he speaks his next words. "I want to possess you, and you'll love every minute of it."

And with that nuclear bomb of a statement, he heads for the bathroom. A moment later I hear the shower turn on, and my knees finally give out on me.

I fall onto the bed, my entire body trembling at the dark promise in Ajax's voice. I feel that tingle racing up and down my spine again—and again it's not fear I feel.

chapter
five

Olivia

I hate to admit it, but even though Ajax doesn't let me go anywhere without him and keeps me basically holed up inside wherever the hell we are, I don't feel like a captive. He stays with me the entire time, talking to me, helping me find myself.

He asks me pointed questions about my likes and dislikes, and it's reminiscent of when I used to sneak out to talk to him. The only thing is now we're not having to look over our shoulders so that my parents don't discover it.

And despite the hungry way his eyes rove over me, he hasn't so much as kissed me again, though every night he sleeps with his arms banded around me like steel, and I can feel his huge erection pressing against my ass.

But he doesn't try anything. I don't know if he's leading me into a false sense of security before he makes his move or if he's genuinely trying to make me comfortable, or if he's just trying to drive me insane.

He doesn't even have to touch me for my body to start burning with desire. All he has to do is gaze at me with that look in his eyes, and I feel like I'm going to spontaneously combust.

In three days, my defenses start to come down. I forget to be angry with him. I find myself laughing at things he says more. I start appreciating the way his eyes crinkle in the corners when he smiles after having made me laugh.

I remember now why I used to sneak out to talk to him. Ajax is fascinating. He makes me laugh, and he really listens to me. I don't think anyone has ever seen me the way he does. He notices every little thing about me. Things I never noticed about myself—like the way I let my hair hang down in front of my shoulder to hide my face when I become uncomfortable. I never realized I did that until he told me I did.

And we have the same taste in movies. Every night he puts on an old black-and-white film. We watch them together, getting lost in the magic of another time.

It's amazing how comfortable I am with him. My mouth drops open in wonder whenever he finally takes me outside and I see that we're in a little cabin in the woods. The interior of the cabin is modern, yet the outside looks so rustic. Judging by the inside of the house, though, I never would have guessed we were in a cabin in the middle of the freaking woods.

I would have thought we were in any house in the city, but no. We're in a wooded area, and again, that's something that should scare me because we look to be off the grid. There's no one around in sight, yet I find it peaceful instead.

We sit on the hanging swing on his porch and listen to the birds chirp and the bees hum. Ajax even shows me how to make sugar water to go in the hummingbird feeder he has hanging up on his front porch, and we sit there and watch the hummingbirds drink the nectar from the feeder.

I'm startled to admit that I can see myself spending the rest of my life like this—with Ajax, his arm draped behind me on the big swing as I sit next to him.

Against my better judgment, I allow myself to relax and lean my body against the crook of his arm. Ajax stills for a moment, but then I feel his big hand on my shoulder as he pulls me in to settle me closer to him. I feel the pleasure wafting off of him, and it humbles me to know that my presence can make him so happy.

I see the adoring way his eyes follow every move I make, and it causes my stomach to flutter with a thousand tiny butterflies.

I still feel the way I did the first time I ever talked to him. Ajax might be a felon. He might seem dangerous to the rest of the world, but he would never hurt me.

That's why I finally get up the courage to ask him what he was sent to prison for.

We're sitting on the swing, and I'm laying with my head in the crook of his neck when I pop the question.

His body tenses, but I don't take it back. I think if he thought it was okay to watch me without my knowledge and to kidnap me, then the least he can do is share his history with me. I'm not going to judge him. I just want to know more about the man whom I'm spending so much time with. He knows basically everything there is to know about me now. It's only fair I know more about him, and I'm prepared to argue that if he doesn't want to open up.

Ajax is quiet for a long moment before he finally sighs and speaks, "I had a little sister."

My heart instantly clenches for him at his use of the past tense—had. I don't interrupt him, though I'm burning with questions already. I let him tell it at his own pace.

"She was beautiful, smart, funny. Everyone loved her. She saw the good in everyone." His eyes flick down at me and soften. "Kind of like you do."

Then he looks back up, gazing out into nothing as he goes on, his jaw hardening, "She was trusting—too trusting—and that trusting nature of hers ultimately got her in trouble. She trusted the wrong person, and he raped her." His voice becomes gravelly before he clears it and goes on, "He raped her and beat her so badly that she didn't survive the attack."

I feel his hand tightening on my shoulder. I can practically feel the pain radiating off him. It's still raw, and I want so much to take it away, to ease it for him.

"The police couldn't find out who did it, so I did their job for them. I found out who did it, and when I did, I took vengeance into my own hands."

"You didn't go to the police with the information?" I surmise.

His jaw clenches. "Why would I? The incompetent fuckers couldn't figure out who did it. I certainly didn't trust them to see justice done. Too many criminals have slipped through the cracks with a good lawyer, and this guy," Ajax snorts, "he was rich. One of the upper crust. He definitely would have had a good lawyer. He'd have probably skated free, and I couldn't have that. I wasn't going to leave anything to chance, so I took care of it myself."

"You killed him," I say it, so he doesn't have to.

He gives a curt nod before he meets my eyes. "I'm not gonna lie to you, Olivia. I don't regret it. In fact, I wish I could dig him back up, bring him back to life, and kill him all over again."

I can hear the anger in his voice, and again, I should probably be scared knowing that I'm sitting in the presence of a murderer, but I'm not. I actually understand. I don't have any siblings, but I have people in my life I love, and if someone hurt them, I can understand how he would want to make sure they paid.

His baby sister, no less. I feel my throat tighten. Hot tears prick my eyes. I feel like I'm speaking around a lump in my throat when I ask, "How did you—?"

Ajax apparently anticipates my question because he interrupts me with, "I got out on a technicality. Turns out the arrest warrant was never properly signed, and the lawyer who did my appeal found what the shitty public defender didn't. They had to release me even though they didn't want to."

He looks down at me now, his eyes burning into me. "I may be a convicted murderer, Olivia, but I swear on my sister's grave I would never hurt you. I would give my life to protect you. All I want is for you to be safe. And happy." His eyes heat as he adds, "And mine."

My heart skips a beat. Ajax has been transparent with me from the beginning. He hasn't pushed me for anything physical, but he's made it very clear what he wants.

When I don't speak, he lets out a self-deprecating laugh. "You're probably terrified of me now, aren't you?"

A few of my tears spill over, and his lips thin as he wipes them away. He looks like he regrets telling me the truth, but I shake my head and seek to set his mind at ease. "No, I'm not afraid of you. I've never been afraid of you. I could always tell you're a good man underneath it all."

His eyes are brown flames blazing down into mine. "You're not a monster, Ajax," I tell him as I lift a shaking hand to touch his cheek.

He closes his eyes and tilts his head into my touch like a dog starved for affection, and that image sears itself on my brain. My heart breaks for him. He had his sister ripped away from him, and he sought justice, and now he's ostracized from society for it.

No, this man isn't a monster. He's a champion. A warrior who's willing to go to war for the people he loves.

"Ajax," I whisper his name, my voice shaky. His eyes snap open to blaze down into mine again.

We both hold our breath for a moment, and then I let the words tumble out before I can chicken out. "Make me yours?"

chapter
six

Ajax

My head spins as I look down at my beautiful, blue-eyed angel. My hand flexes where it's still curled around her shoulder, and it takes all the strength within me not to cover her body with mine and take her like a savage here on this swing.

"Are you sure?" My voice comes out as a growl.

Olivia licks her lips, and her cheeks turn pink.

I cup her face in my hand. Her pretty blue eyes flutter up to meet mine. "Because I swear to god, Olivia, once I have you, that's it. You're mine. Forever. There won't be any turning back. I'll be incapable of it." My throat tightens, and I choke on the last sentence.

Olivia holds my eyes as she nods her head. "I understand. I want you, Ajax."

And that's what does it. Hearing the object of my obsession admitting she wants me snaps the last ounce of control I've been holding onto all week.

I haul her into my lap, and then my lips are on hers. She opens to me immediately, her honeyed lips just as sweet as the last time I kissed her. I find her tongue and tangle it with mine while I fist my fingers in the honeyed tresses of her hair.

Honey. Everything about her is sweet as honey. Maybe that's why I always call her that.

"Fuck, Olivia," I groan into her mouth as I grab her hips and drag her hot little mound up and down my aching length. I'm straining in my pants, dying to get to her wet heat. I already know before I reach between us she's soaking wet.

Slow down, my mind tells me. Savor this moment. Olivia is giving herself to you. Cherish her. Worship her.

But my body has other ideas. My hands shake as I slip that cherry-covered dress over her head and fling it onto the porch. I yank the cups of her bra down and marvel at her pink nipples. They're drawn up into little pebbles and begging to be sucked, and I'm dying to taste them.

I swirl my tongue around one and then the other. Olivia moans my name, her head falling back. I move my mouth up to the creamy column of her throat to lick and suck on the sweet flesh there. She jumps when I nip at her neck, but I lick the sting away and can't resist sucking on the tender skin there, pulling the blood up to pool beneath the surface.

I know it makes me a caveman, but I need to mark her. It's like I'm no longer in control of my senses. All my primal instincts have taken over, and they're screaming at me to claim, claim, claim! Claim my woman.

Her hands are tugging at my shirt. I know what she wants, and who am I to deny her anything? I pull back from her just long to rip it off. Fire floods my veins at the way her eyes trail over my bare chest, appreciating what she sees. She reaches out and trails her fingers over it down to my stomach.

I groan and still her hand when it nears the band of my shorts. I don't want this to be over too quickly.

Before I can do anything else, she leans in and places her sweet lips against my chest. I jump as if I've been electrocuted, my hands tunneling into her hair to cradle her against me as she peeks up at me innocently while kissing all over my chest.

Fuck! A sound something like a bear rumbles up out

of me, and then I'm kissing her again, my lips sliding over hers, our tongues tangling together.

Olivia kisses me back just as passionately, her hands spearing into my hair like mine does hers. We're breathing the same breaths, lost in the moment together. Fuck, I could stay like this with her forever.

But she begins humping her hips against me, and I hiss in a breath at the friction that almost has me coming in my pants immediately. "Olivia, honey," I grit out as I place a hand on her hip to hold her still.

She whimpers and looks up at me shyly. "I'm sorry. I've never..." she bites her lip, and I bend down to place a tender kiss on her lips before nipping her puffy bottom lip myself.

"You're not doing anything wrong, honey," I reassure her. "I'm just so fucking wound up for you. I want this to last. I want to make your first time good for you."

"I want to be good for you too," she tells me in her husky little voice.

Fuuuck. "You are, sweet baby." I kiss her forehead. "Everything about you is perfect. There's no way you could ever disappoint me."

"Even though I'm..." she trails off.

"A virgin?" I supply before I let out a chuckle of relief. "Especially because of that. You have no idea how happy it makes me that I'll be the only man to ever be inside you."

"So you're glad I'm a virgin?" She looks unsure.

"Ecstatic," I tell her truthfully. "Was that your first orgasm the other night?"

Her cheeks turn pink, and she tries to hide from me by letting her hair fall in front of her shoulders. I tip her chin back up to me. "Was it?" I press her.

"Yes," she finally breathes her admittance. "I tried to touch myself before, but I never could...I couldn't..."

"You could never make yourself come," I clarify.

She presses her lips together and nods.

I speak close to her ear, my heart pounding when I ask her my next question. "What made that time different?"

Her breath hitches. I already know the answer, but I want to hear her admit it anyway.

"I was thinking about you."

I cup her face and look into her blue eyes. They're shining with vulnerability. She's baring her naked soul to me, and it's more glorious than anything in this world. Fuck diamonds, fuck a sunset. None of it compares to what I see in her eyes right now.

I can't take it anymore and crash my lips back onto hers. "I want to devour you," I tell her in between kisses.

"I want every part of you. Every thought. Every breath. Everything, Olivia."

She trembles in my arms, and I stand and carry her inside. I need her laid out on the bed for what I have planned for her.

The feeling of her arms and legs wrapped around me as I carry her is so good I don't want to put her down, but the way she whimpers and wiggles against my cock has primitive needs overriding all others right now. My princess needs relief, and I'm going to give it to her.

I lay her out on the bed before me and slip off her little red panties before I drop to my knees before her. I nudge her legs open and feel a jet of precum shoot from my tip at the first sight I get of her pretty pink pussy. It's glistening with juices and looks tighter than a motherfucker.

Fuuuck. Pink. The pretty pink of her virgin pussy. That's my new favorite color.

I lean in, letting her scent tease my nostrils before I dive in, licking her from gash to clit. She jumps when I find her clit and suck on it. I feel the spasms shooting through her as she screams out with each roll of my tongue over her swollen pearl.

I press a finger into her until I reach the barrier of her hymen. I pump it in and out and slowly add another finger, trying to ready her for my cock. I'm not breaking her cherry yet, though. My cock will be the one to do the honors of that. I want to be looking deep into her eyes when I make her mine in every way.

Only when I feel her pussy clenching around my fingers as she comes do I pull back, watching her as she convulses with my fingers still buried inside her.

Her head is thrown back, hair splayed out as she tosses her head back and forth wildly, a thin sheen of perspiration making her skin glow.

I've never seen anything more beautiful than my Olivia in this moment.

She's still coming down from her orgasm when I shuck my pants off and fist my throbbing length. My tip is purple and angry looking, and I'm so hard I have to bend the fucker down to line it up with Olivia's still-coming pussy.

"Look at me, honey," I coax her as I start to press up into her. Even with her just coming, she's still tighter than a fist, and I grit my teeth as I plow slowly forward.

Her blue eyes flash to mine. Her hands fly up to grip my shoulders as I continue to feed my inches slowly into her.

"Ajax," she whispers my name tremulously.

I swallow at the look on her face. She feels it too. This insane soul-winding current between us. This is more than just sex. This is our souls joining together as one.

Tears glisten in her eyes as she asks me tremulously. "Do you love me?"

I'm so shocked at her words I go completely still.

"Oh god, I'm so sorry for asking you that!" She covers her face with her hands in mortification, and my heart swells damn near to bursting within me.

I lean down and kiss her hands before I pry them gently away from her face, my heart full with everything I feel for her. My Olivia.

I kiss her forehead, her cheeks, and her nose before I finally kiss her lips, taking my time, letting her feel everything I feel for her in my lips.

When I finally pull back from her, my cock still just partly inside her and aching to go deeper, she's looking up at me softly. "Of course, I love you, Olivia. I'm fucking crazy about you. You're my entire world. You just don't know, honey."

She smiles at me then, and I'm surprised I don't have a heart attack at the words she speaks next. "I love you too, Ajax. I think I always have. I think that's why I was so drawn to you. Is that possible? To love someone before you even know them?"

She's looking at me so curiously like she trusts me to

have all the answers to the universe. "I don't know, honey, but I feel the same way."

She lifts her hips to me in offering. "Do it," she orders me sweetly.

"It'll hurt," I warn her, already hating the thought of hurting her but determined that I'll make up for it a hundred times over.

She nods. "I don't care. I want to make you feel good."

I hold her eyes as I pull back and then slam the rest of the way inside her. She cries out at the pinch, but then I'm engulfed in her hot heat, and I'm fighting to keep from busting inside her immediately.

She's clinging to me, and my jaw is clenched as she pulses around me. She wiggles underneath me, and I groan as I slide inside her. "Fuck, baby." I pull out and push back in. She moans.

"Are you okay?" I ask her, my voice sounding labored.

She nods. "Yes, it's starting to feel good," she admits with a blush.

I cup her face between my hands and stare into her eyes as I begin pushing deeper into her. Her mouth falls open in a silent "o" as I pick up the pace.

My heart is hammering in my chest, and I become more feral with each stroke until I'm rutting into her hard and fast. Her little tits are jiggling, and she bites her lip as she holds eye contact with me.

I'm so far gone I can't think straight. "Got me locked down over this pussy," I tell her. "You know that, honey? I'm yours, sweet baby. Now and forever."

"And I'm yours," she moans as she circles her hands around my neck. "I'm sorry I ever fought it, Ajax."

I grab her ass and angle her up so I can hit her even deeper. She screams when I find her g spot and begin stabbing it repeatedly. Oh fuck, yeah, I can't wait to feel her coming on my cock. "You going to give me that sweet cum because I've got such a big nut to give you, baby. Been saving all this cum up just for you, sweetheart."

I feel the tingle starting at the base of my spine. My balls are churning. I'm right there.

"Fuck, Olivia!" I roar just as I feel her pussy clench my cock hard.

"Ajax!" she screams my name, and once I feel her pussy fluttering around my length, I'm gone.

I don't hold back. I cry out like a wounded animal as my hot release begins to fill her pussy.

I hold on to her hips as I jam myself inside her to the hilt and hold myself there, trying to flood her sweet cunt with as much of my seed as I can.

I come so much I can feel my release leaking out

around us on the bed, and when I give a couple more pumps to finish off my load, the squelching sound of our wet sexes fills the room.

I manage to catch myself before I fall on her in a heap, angling my body so that I fall onto my side. I pull her with me, keeping myself still buried inside her.

I band my arms tight about her and bury my head in her hair, inhaling her sweet honey scent.

A rush of possessiveness swells my chest. She's perfect.

And she's mine.

I'm never going to let her go.

chapter
seven

Olivia

Ajax was right. I have more freedom here with him than I've ever had in my entire life. There's a type of freedom to submitting to what we both wanted from the beginning and not worrying about what I should want or what I'm expected to do. When Ajax said I was just too afraid to make that jump, he was right. He knew I needed a push, so in a funny way, by kidnapping me, Ajax really saved me.

He saved me from a life of mediocrity, of doing what my parents want just to make them happy—whether I'm happy or not.

I still love my parents, and I don't hold anything

against them. I know deep in my heart that they only wanted the best for me, but their dreams aren't the same as mine.

I still don't really know what my dreams are—just that wherever they take me, Ajax will be by my side. And at this point, that's all I really care about.

So, yes, there's freedom in submitting to Ajax, in trusting him to take care of everything. I know I'm safe —loved—here with him.

Ajax doesn't pressure me to figure out what I'm going to do with the rest of my life right now. He's content to let me just exist and float along with what we have going on—like I'm a bottle in the waves of the ocean.

It's nice to take my foot off the gas for once. My whole life everything has been planned. Trying to get straight A's in school, doing extracurricular activities, everything was building up to college and then a successful career. Even if I wasn't sure what I wanted that career to be, I'm sure my mom and dad would have hand-picked one for me if I'd let them.

But Ajax assures me there's no rush and that if I never want to do anything, that he's more than willing to take care of the both of us. Of course, I think I'd go crazy if I didn't do anything, but I'm just not sure what that something I really want to do is yet. I've never really stopped and thought about what I want before. I've always just done what was expected of me, and Ajax is the first person who saw that in me. So, for now, I enjoy going through the motions of the day with Ajax.

He must have had some money saved up—at least enough to be able to take some time off—because he hasn't left me alone at all since we've been here. I go to bed every night wrapped up in his arms after he thoroughly makes love to me. Sometimes he makes love to me soft and slow, worshiping me and making me feel like a revered goddess, and other times, he gets me on all fours and holds me up against the wall as he rails me.

I don't know which I prefer. I love them both, and Ajax always seems to know exactly what kind of loving I need.

Of course, as all good things do, our perfect little bubble comes to an end one day.

We're sitting on the porch swing, as we often do in the evening, watching the sun go down when Ajax's phone buzzes. He's not on his phone a lot, though he does check it periodically. I don't know what he does on it, and I don't ask. I don't want to be one of those prying girlfriends.

I glance over at his face as he opens up his phone, and I immediately get a bad feeling in the pit of my stomach when I see his jaw tighten. His nostrils flare, and he swallows as he grips the phone in his hand hard. I feel his hand flex where it's gripping my shoulder, his arm that's wrapped around me going taut.

"Is everything okay?" I ask him tentatively, concerned with the sudden change in his demeanor.

He looks up at me with a tight expression. "No," he admits, "but don't worry about it, honey. It will be."

I open my mouth to ask what he means, but he takes my hand and stands up, pulling me along with him. "I have something I need to take care of. I'm going to take you back home while I do it."

There's a new urgency in his voice that has alarm bells tripping off in my head. "What?"

"It won't be for long, Olivia, but trust that everything I'm doing is for your own good. There's nothing for you to worry about, honey." He strokes my cheek.

I frown up at him, but I can already tell by the set of his jaw that he's resolute in his decision. Still, I want answers. "What's going on? You can't just order me to go home and not tell me what's going on and expect me not to worry. This isn't like you at all, Ajax. What did you see on your phone?"

Ajax's lips press into a thin line, and when he speaks, he speaks from between clenched teeth. "Don't worry about it. I'll take care of it."

I can't stop the hurt from washing over me, so I lash

out in anger. "Oh, so that's how it is? You want me to share everything with you, but you won't do the same. Do you not trust me?"

Ajax huffs out an aggravated breath and runs a hand through his hair. "It's not that, Olivia. I'm just trying to protect you."

"I'm a grown woman," I snap back. "I can handle it." My voice turns pleading. "Just let me help."

"You can help by doing as you're told." His eyes flash, and I shrink back from the harshness of his tone.

He instantly looks apologetic and grabs my shoulders to pull me in for a hug. He breathes out heavily like he's trying to calm himself. "I'm sorry, honey. I didn't mean to snap at you like that."

He lets out another heavy sigh before he holds his phone out to me and presses play on a clip.

It shows a bald-headed man covered in tattoos rummaging through what looks like an apartment. I look up at Ajax inquisitively, and he answers my unspoken question. "That's my apartment back in the city."

My hands fly up to cover my mouth as fear laces through me. "Oh my gosh! Do you know the guy?"

Ajax's jaw hardens again before he shakes his head. "I've never met him in person, but I know who he is."

I stare at him, waiting for him to reveal more.

He regards me for a long moment before he finally admits, "He's the brother of the man I killed."

A chill goes through me as I gasp and turn fearful eyes up to Ajax. "He's out for revenge," I surmise.

A muscle in Ajax's jaw flexes before he nods his head curtly. "Probably." He pulls me close again and strokes his hand over my head like I'm a frightened animal he's trying to soothe. "But you don't need to worry about anything, honey. I'm going to take care of everything, but in order for me to focus, I need to make sure you're safe. You understand that, honey?"

I tilt my head up to look at him. I chew on my lip as I look into his caramel chocolate eyes. "I'm worried about you," I finally admit.

His eyes soften as he looks down at me. He strokes his thumb over my cheek before he kisses me gently on the forehead. "I'll be okay, honey. I can take care of myself, but I need to know that you're safe while I'm doing what I have to do, so that's why I want you to be a good girl and listen to me. I'm going to take you home, and you're going to stay in the house with your mother and father. Don't come out for anything until I come back to get you."

I shake my head, tears pooling in my eyes at the thought of him getting hurt. "No." I shake my head. "I can help—"

Ajax interrupts me with a stern look. "This is non-negotiable, Olivia. I don't want to be parted from you either. Not for a second. You know that. But I'm not taking any risks when it comes to your safety. Let me take care of this, and I'll be back for you as soon as I can."

I press my lips together as the tears spill over. I can tell that no amount of arguing will budge Ajax's stance, so I keep my mouth shut even as a heavy weight descends on me.

I won't give him any trouble. I'll let him take me home to my parents, but if he thinks I'm going to sit idly by while his life is in danger, he's wrong. There might not be much I can do, but I have to do something. Ajax saved me from myself. I love him, and I'll die if anything happens to him.

"Good girl," he praises me before he places a gentle kiss on my lips, obviously taking my silence as acceptance.

I don't know what I'm going to do, but the wheels in my mind are churning. I can't lose him now.

I can't.

Ajax

I always knew the fucker who raped and murdered my sister had a brother. Carlos Dennings. That's his name. He was locked up whenever I killed his brother, but I've kept an eye on him since his release. I've been vigilant, making sure he wasn't going to come after me. I've always been one who was prepared for every eventuality.

The man didn't seem to be out for vengeance. I don't know if he and his brother were close. At first, I thought maybe he didn't give a shit since he never came after me. I don't know what's possessed him to start coming after me now—if maybe he's just been biding his time up until now—but I'll take care of it. I'm not going to have anyone ruin what I have with Olivia. Now that I finally have her, nothing is going to jeopardize that. I can understand the guy being pissed about his brother, but I have to wonder if he knew what kind of man his brother was.

I don't really give a fuck either way because no one is going to threaten Olivia, and as much as I hate to send her back to her parents, I'll do whatever I have to do to keep her safe.

I look down at my princess where she sits in the passenger seat of my SUV with her little brow furrowed. If it wasn't for the anxiety coursing through me, I would smile at her demeanor. She thinks I don't know her well enough to know that she's plotting something in those pretty blue eyes of hers. She has absolutely no intention of staying put like I told her, and while it warms my heart to know that she truly does care about me enough to worry about me, her safety comes before anything.

That's why when we get to her house, I get out of the car with her.

Her eyes widen as she watches me step out of the driver's seat. "What are you doing?" she asks me, her voice slightly panicky.

I walk around to her door and open it, holding my hand out to help her from the vehicle. She places her tiny hand in my palm, and those familiar tingles shoot throughout my entire system. Will she always affect me like this? Something tells me she will.

"Walking you to your door," I tell her.

She shakes he head and is getting ready to argue with me—I can tell—but I shake my head.

"I need to have a few words with your father."

Olivia's eyes widen, and then her protests set in, "Ajax, no—"

I cut her off with a quick kiss to her lips. Although it's quick, I kiss her deeply, putting all the love and obsession I feel for her into the kiss until I feel her melt against me.

Once I've kissed her into submission, I walk her to the door and knock on it.

Her mother opens it, her eyes going wide when she sees her daughter. "Olivia!" the older copy of my princess exclaims before she pulls her daughter into her for a fierce hug, her eyes glancing over Olivia's shoulder to me questioningly.

"I need to speak to your husband," I tell her, but I already see the man coming up behind Olivia and her mother. I see the relief pass through his eyes as they land on his daughter before they cut up to me and narrow suspiciously.

"Mr. Carson," I nod my head cordially at him.

The man gives the briefest nod in return, but he doesn't speak my name. That's okay. I don't need the man to like me. I just need him to keep his daughter safe long enough for me to sort all this out.

"Can I have a word with you?" I ask him frankly.

Again, he doesn't speak. He just studies me before he steps out onto the porch with me, closing his wife and daughter up behind us. The way he doesn't invite me into his home doesn't go unnoticed by me, but again, I don't give a fuck. I'm not here to make friends with him. Of course, it'd be more ideal if he liked me, for Olivia's sake anyway.

But I'm not looking for a father figure. If he doesn't like me, I don't really give a fuck. I'll always show him respect simply because he's my girl's father, but at the same time, I'm not giving Olivia up for anything—not now that she's recognized her feelings for me and gave herself to me so sweetly.

"So...you're the reason my daughter ran off." He doesn't ask it as a question. He simply states it as a fact.

I'm just as blunt in my answer. "Yes," I confirm. No need to tell the man that I kidnapped her right out from underneath his nose. I'm sure that wouldn't be a good way to start off our relationship.

The man's jaw ticks as he stares at me before he

accuses, "So, I guess you got what you wanted, and you're bringing her back."

My own jaw clenches as anger flares up in my chest, hot and heavy. I speak to him from between clenched teeth. I don't really have time for this shit. "That is the last time you speak about her like that in my presence," I warn him. I don't care if the man is her father. No one talks about my Olivia that way.

"I'm in love with your daughter," I tell him, "and I intend on marrying her."

He scoffs as he crosses his arms. "Well, if you're looking for my blessing, then—"

"With all due respect, sir, that's not why I'm here."

He narrows his eyes at me again. "What is it then?"

I don't beat around the bush. "Long story short. I have to take care of something that could potentially be dangerous, and I don't want your daughter anywhere in harm's way. I'm trusting you to keep her here. Under no circumstances do you allow her to leave."

I watch Carson's face go from indignant at being told want to do to ashen in the span of minutes.

He looks at me guardedly. "So you're trying to protect her?" he grunts.

"Yes," I confirm. "She's not happy with my decision to have her come back and stay with you while I do this, but her safety is the most important thing to me, and I believe you'll do your best to keep her safe." I'm not kissing the man's ass. I truly believe that next to me, in her father's care is the safest place for her to be.

Something like respect flashes in his eyes as he looks me over again before he says gruffly, "She's my daughter. Of course I'll watch over her."

I turn to leave, but Carson's voice calls out to me. "I just need to know one thing before you go."

I half-turn to look at him. His jaw hardens again. "You say you love my daughter and you intend to marry her. As a father, I think I have the right to know what kind of man she's getting involved with. I realize she's eighteen, and I can't control her choices. She's definitely made some lately that I don't approve of." His eyes skirt over me again. Message taken. He doesn't approve of me. Oh well, it won't change a thing. I'm not letting her go.

He finally gets to the point. "Are you a cold-blooded killer?"

I stare at him stoically, though I am admittedly taken aback by his question. In his own way, he's asking me for an explanation of my prison stent, which is more than most people have ever done. I know he's only doing it because of my involvement with his daughter, but still.

I tell him the truth. "I'm a convicted murderer, and I'm not going to lie to you and tell you I regret it. I would do it all over again."

He doesn't blink as he lets me go on. "A man raped my sister so viciously she didn't survive the attack."

His face blanches. I don't have to spell it out for him. He's smart enough to put two and two together.

He holds my eyes as the knowledge sinks in before he asks, "Are you involved in anything dangerous?"

Again, I know what he's asking me. If I engage in any sort of criminal behavior that will put his daughter in jeopardy. It's a fair question, one that any self-respecting father would ask the man who wants to marry his daughter.

I shake my head. "No, sir. Never have been. Never will be. All I care about is Olivia and making her happy and keeping her safe."

The man stares at me for a few more moments as if he's trying to assess if I'm telling him the truth, and then I see respect light in his eyes.

He holds his hand out to me, and I shake it firmly. Neither of us speaks any more words, but we don't need them. I see the message clear as day in his eyes. He respects me for avenging my sister. He'd have done the same thing for someone he loved. He can sense that I'm genuine when it comes to his daughter and that I'll take care of her.

And really, that's the most that any father can want for the man who claims his daughter, isn't it?

"Do what you gotta do, son." He nods at me again.

I nod my head in return, a strange tightening taking place in my chest at the acceptance in that word.

Son.

Now that's a word I never thought I would hear Olivia's father calling me.

Ajax

I frown as I follow the trail Dennings left me. Some of the signs are a little too obvious. It's almost like he wanted me to find him. Maybe he just wants the confrontation. I don't know, but I'm ready to take care of this because I'm already missing Olivia like crazy.

I've got my pistol and plenty of knives strapped to me as I make my way into the seedy-looking neighborhood this fucker lives in. I don't see any sign of security at his address, and the door is unlocked, which sets my senses on high alert. Somehow before I ever step foot into the space, I already know he won't be there. A quick sweep of the space confirms my suspicions. My heart is already hammering in dread when I find a hastily scrawled piece of paper taped to the inside of the door.

You took my brother from me. I'm going to take the only person you care about from you.

My vision goes red, and my chest tightens before a roar that sounds inhuman even to my own ears bursts up out of me. Olivia! Fuck, he's going after Olivia. It's the culmination of all my worst fears.

Fuck! This was all a trap to get Olivia alone. I've been so wrapped in Olivia I became lax in my watch of Dennings. I thought he was just after me. I was hoping he didn't even know about her. I should have known better. I should have known he'd try to hit me where he knew it would hurt the most.

I take off speeding down the highway to Olivia's parents' place. I already know how flimsy Carson's security is. It was a joke for me to get by. It'll be an easy hack for anyone who's been in the pen before, and I know Dennings has. Carson's security is a joke.

I'm beating myself up for not having his number so I can call him and warn him. Olivia doesn't have a phone on her either.

"Fuck!" I scream again as I pound the steering wheel.

The street is completely dark when I get back to the Carsons' place. A quick survey of the perimeter shows me that someone has already disabled the security system. Panic grips me as I make my way toward the back door, desperately praying that I find Olivia and her parents unharmed.

The house is quiet, which could be a good sign or a bad one. I immediately hasten toward Olivia's room. There are no lights on in the house at all except for a few softly burning lamps that the family always keeps on.

I'm hoping everyone is asleep and that Dennings isn't here yet. I'm going to get Olivia and take her someplace safe. I'll alert Carson to the situation so he can protect himself and his wife.

My heart about bursts out of my chest whenever I reach the top of the stairway and turn toward Olivia's door. It's halfway open, and I see a figure looming closer to her.

I react on instinct, barreling through the door and throwing myself at the man. I knock him off balance, and we tumble to the floor, fists flying as we fight like rabid animals.

Olivia scurries up and turns on the bedside lamp, screaming when she sees the commotion going on in her floor. I vaguely hear footsteps pounding up the steps, and then Carson is there at her door.

I'm pleased to see that the man jumps into action, running straight to Olivia. He tries to usher her from the room, but my stubborn little Olivia is resisting him.

"No, Dad!" she screams. "I can't leave Ajax!"

I see the knife glinting in the other man's hand as he tries to stab it into me.

Olivia's scream distracts me, and I glance over at her to make sure she's okay. A hiss out a breath as I feel the knife slice into my shoulder.

"Olivia, go!" I yell at her as Dennings succeeds in pulling a gun out of his pocket. He starts lifting it, pointing it right at my chest, and the only thought in my head is what's going to happen to Olivia if this man blows me to smithereens.

Before I can even lunge at him to try to wrestle the gun from him, a deafening pop sounds out in the room.

Dennings' eyes go wide, and his gun clatters to the floor, followed swiftly by his body, blood pooling in the center of his chest.

I turn to see Carson holding a smoking gun. Olivia comes running straight for me, flinging herself into my arms and sobbing wildly.

I clutch her to me tightly and stroke my fingers through her hair, soothing myself as much as her, relieved that she wasn't harmed.

"Oh my god, Ajax! He almost killed you!" She's hysterical, but I hold her close, speaking softly to her to calm her down.

"It's okay, honey. I'm fine. Nothing will ever take me

away from you, my sweet girl. I'm so sorry. So sorry." I kiss her forehead, and she tightens her arms around me.

"You have nothing to be sorry for," she sniffles. "This isn't your fault."

My throat is tight as I hug her to me again, probably too hard, but the thought of losing her fills me with fear. "If it hadn't been for me, he wouldn't have come after you at all, Olivia."

Olivia is already shaking her head in protest.

I look up to find her father watching us. I nod at him. "Thank you, sir." I owe Olivia's father my life, and that's a debt I won't take lightly. I realize Dennings probably would have shot me if it hadn't been for Carson.

Olivia looks up at her father as if she's just now remembering he's still there. She pulls away from me, and I reluctantly release her. She runs over to her father and wraps her arms around him. "Thank you, Daddy. Thank you," she sobs into his chest now. "Thank you for saving the man I love." Her voice catches on the words.

Carson looks from his daughter to me and then back again before he releases her and then gives me another one of those respectful nods. "My daughter is right. This wasn't your fault. You risked your life to save her."

"It was a setup—" I explain, but Carson holds up a hand to silence me.

"Don't try to accept any of the blame. You put yourself in danger to save us all, but most especially my daughter, and I'll forever be grateful to you for that."

"I don't know what would have happened if you hadn't gotten here when you did..."His voice wavers. "I see now that you really would do anything to protect my daughter."

Carson clears his throat before adding. "I owe you an apology. I misjudged you. You did what you had to do—in both situations."

I know he's reaffirming to me he understands about my murder conviction.

"That's the mark of a true man," he adds gruffly, "and I could ask no more of the man who wants to marry my daughter."

Olivia turns wide eyes to me. "Marry?" she whispers.

I go over to her and take her hands in between mine, needing to touch her to reassure myself that she's indeed safe. "I may have already told your father I intend to marry you."

"But you haven't even asked me," she whispers.

Her father interjects with, "I think he's asking you now, child."

This isn't really how I planned to do this, but I can't wait any longer. I kiss Olivia's knuckles tenderly. I'd love to kiss her lips, but I'm aware that her father is still watching us, and while the man may have accepted me now, he could change his mind if he sees me ravishing his daughter right in front of him.

"Olivia, you know how much I love you, the lengths I would go to for you. I want to spend the rest of my life protecting you. Marry me."

Olivia smiles at me tearfully before she whispers "yes"—even though my proposal wasn't really a question—and throws herself back in my arms. I hug her close to me, stroking my hands over her hair again, that strange tightness in my throat again.

"Well, I suppose we need to catch your mother up on everything and tell her she's getting a new son-in-law," Carson comments dryly just as the flashing lights of the police stream through the window.

Olivia wraps her arms around my neck, and I whisper against her ear, "Are you okay, honey?"

She nods. "I'm always okay, as long as I'm with you."

And I can't help it. I can't hold off any longer. Her father may be standing there, but I'll die if I don't kiss her.

So I do.

epilogue

Eight Months Later

Olivia

I **SMILE** and run my fingers through my husband's hair as he kisses my swollen belly. It's just one of the things that makes my heart melt about him. He was ecstatic when he found out I was pregnant, and he's always speaking to our child and stroking my belly and kissing it.

Our little one already knows who her daddy is if the way she kicks every time he speaks to her is any indication, and he loves it. The boyish grin that lights his face every time she shows out for him makes my heart melt with joy.

It's no wonder I got pregnant so soon. Ajax and I never use protection. He said he couldn't stand the thought of anything being between us, and that's okay with me because I felt the same way.

I finally decided what I want to do with my life—at least for now. I want to be a wife and mother. First and foremost, I'm going to take care of our baby until she goes to school, and in the meantime, I'll help Ajax with his business. I'll help secure him new clients and book his appointments for him. If I decide I want to do something else whenever our little girl goes to school, I can. I have time to figure it all out. There's no rush on anything.

Because if seeing Ajax's life hanging in the balance taught me anything, it's that life is short and you need to spend it with the ones you love.

I think my parents feel the same way because they've completely accepted Ajax. We have Sunday brunch with them every week, and it always brings tears to my eyes when I hear the way my father calls Ajax "son."

I think Ajax really proved himself when he put his life at risk to save mine. He definitely gained my father's respect, and he's so sweet to my mother that she can't help but adore him just like I do.

"I think I've decided on a name for our baby girl," I tell him.

I smile at how fast he sits up and the way he looks at me so intently. His excitement is palpable.

"Yeah?" he prompts me.

Before we had the ultrasound to find out if our baby was a boy or a girl, Ajax and I agreed that if he was a boy, he would name him and if she was a girl, I would name her.

"What have you decided on, honey?" I can hear the anticipation and curiosity in Ajax's deep voice. I know he would be happy with anything that I chose. He agrees with me on nearly everything—unless it's something that puts me or the baby in danger, and according to Ajax, carrying a bag of groceries into the house is dangerous for me and the baby. He won't let me lift a finger to do anything. It was kind of cute at first, but sometimes it gets annoying when he acts like I can't even walk up a flight of stairs and he has to carry me.

"Bree," I say softly. I watch the way his eyes widen with surprise before they melt in chocolate caramel pools. Moisture glistens in them, and he swallows hard as if he's overcome by emotion.

"After your sister," I finish softly.

He doesn't speak. I think he's incapable of it at this moment, and that's okay with me. I can read what his eyes are saying even if he can't voice it.

He wordlessly pulls me close to him in a crushing hug before he kisses me deeply. I kiss him back just as deeply, and as they always do, our kisses turn frantic.

I'm always hot for my husband, so I can't blame it completely on the pregnancy hormones, though they certainly do amp everything up a notch.

We both spear our fingers into each other's hair as he pulls me on top of him to straddle him. He frees himself from his pants and yanks my dress up, pulling my panties to the side so he can slip inside me in one slick thrust.

We growl into each other's mouths as we rock gently together. Sometimes I get frustrated, wanting Ajax to take me harder, but he's such a psycho about my pregnancy. He insists on being slow and gentle, saying he doesn't want to hurt the baby, and no amount of coaxing on my part will convince him that a little bit of harder sex won't hurt our child.

Just like he doesn't take any chances with my safety, he won't take any with our child either. As frustrated as I get, it only makes me love him even more. He's going to be a wonderful father. Just like he's a wonderful husband.

We move slowly against each other, staring into each other's eyes as we continue to kiss and stroke each other until our release crashes all over us. I feel his hot heat spilling up into me, warming me from the inside out. Contentment falls over me until I'm practically purring in his arms.

He tilts my chin up and gives me a languorous, lingering kiss. "Do you know how much I love you?" I feel the rumble of his words through his chest.

I smile up at him. "As much as I love you."

"A man has ever loved a woman as much as I love you," he vows, the melted caramel of his eyes smoldering at me.

"A woman has never loved a man as much as I do you," I insist.

He doesn't argue with me. Instead, he covers my lips with his again, and we both communicate our love to each other with the gliding of our lips together. When we kiss, it's so much more than just a physical sensation. We can feel our souls joining, and it makes me so happy I can hardly contain it.

Tears prick my eyes. When Ajax kidnapped me, he saved my life and captured my heart.

And he still holds my heart in his hands. He always will.

THE END

Connect with Emma!

Visit Emma's website to get a FREE book you can't get anywhere else: www.authoremmabray.com.